Tanzania

Zambia

Malawi

Mozambique

Zimbabwe

To J J, Emily, Audie, and Griz for brightening my world.
To Chelsea for sharing the Malawi adventure.
And to the children of Malawi for broadening my horizons.
—C. R.

To all of the girls finding their place in the world . . . we see you.
—E. Z.

STERLING CHILDREN'S BOOKS
New York

An Imprint of Sterling Publishing Co., Inc.
1166 Avenue of the Americas
New York, NY 10036

ISBN 978-1-4549-2357-2

Library of Congress Cataloging-in-Publication Data

Names: Rose, Carolyn, author. | Zunon, Elizabeth, illustrator.
Title: As big as the sky / by Carolyn Rose ; illustrated by Elizabeth Zunon.
Description: New York, NY : Sterling Publishing Co., Inc., [2019] | Summary:
  Prisca and her brother Caleb have always worked and played together in their village in Malawi, so when
he goes away to school she struggles to find a way to join him. Includes glossary of Chichewa words.
Identifiers: LCCN 2019010219 | ISBN 9781454923572
Subjects: | CYAC: Brothers and sisters—Fiction. | Family
  life—Malawi—Fiction. | Malawi—Fiction.
Classification: LCC PZ7.1.R66916 As 2019 | DDC [E]—dc23

Distributed in Canada by Sterling Publishing Co., Inc.
c/o Canadian Manda Group, 664 Annette Street
Toronto, Ontario M6S 2C8, Canada
Distributed in the United Kingdom by GMC Distribution Services
Castle Place, 166 High Street, Lewes, East Sussex BN7 1XU, England
Distributed in Australia by NewSouth Books
University of New South Wales, Sydney, NSW 2052, Australia

For information about custom editions, special sales, and premium and
corporate purchases, please contact Sterling Special Sales at 800-805-5489
or specialsales@sterlingpublishing.com.

Manufactured in China

Lot #:
2 4 6 8 10 9 7 5 3 1
10/19

sterlingpublishing.com

Cover and interior design by Irene Vandervoort

As Big as the SKY

by CAROLYN ROSE

illustrated by ELIZABETH ZUNON

STERLING CHILDREN'S BOOKS

New York

Can't catch me!" Caleb yelled as he dashed out of sight.

Prisca never could catch him. But she loved the chase. She scrambled past huts and fields, her bare feet skimming over stones. And just as she cornered a fence, he leaped out and pounced.

"*Aaaah!*" she screamed.

"*Heee, hee, hee, heeee!*" Caleb laughed his raucous laugh.

"*Ow, ow, ooowww!*" Prisca howled her joyful howl.

He was her feisty brother, and she was his spunky sister, and their love was as big as the sky.

Life in their village was not all play.

When Prisca wobbled under her heavy bucket, Caleb would grab it. And with a splash and a chuckle, he'd carry it up the steep hill.

When Caleb got sick with malaria, all sweaty and shaky, Prisca would bring him sweet tea and nsima. Then she'd scold the mosquitoes to make him smile.

Together, they pounded corn and swept the yard. They washed the clothes and pulled the weeds.

Then Caleb would yell, "Can't catch me!" and off they'd run.

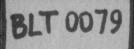

With no good schools for Caleb in the village, it
came time for him to move to Grandma's in Chimwe.
And Prisca cried, "Don't go!"

With a tear in his eye, Caleb called out, "Don't forget
me, Prisca!"

All through the dry season, Prisca yearned for Caleb. There were no cars or buses in the village, and van rides to Chimwe cost 600 kwacha per passenger. Where would she ever get that much money?

Sifting handfuls of dried corn through her fingers, she thought, *I could sell this for 600 kwacha, but then what would Mama and I eat?*

Prisca didn't want to be hungry again like two years earlier, when the crops dried up and all she could think about was her growling stomach.

One day Tewa Tewa, the peddler, came by, calling, "Mwadzuka bwangi, Prisca!"

His bike shimmered with pans and cups, balls and flags, and shiny trinkets of all kinds.

"Good morning, Tewa Tewa!" Prisca cried, handing him a drink.

"Zikomo kwambiri, Prisca! You're so kind!"

Prisca ran her hand along the toys, jingling a bell, spinning a pinwheel, shaking a rattle. Then she stopped.

"Tewa Tewa, I need money to visit my brother. If I make something nice, would you sell it for me?"

"Like what, Prisca?"

"I could paint rocks."

"Paint some and we'll see."

"I will!" Prisca cried.

She ran to the place where she and Caleb had buried
their hidden treasure of rocks. She cleaned them up, painted
them brightly, and gave them to Tewa Tewa.

The next day when Tewa Tewa
returned, Prisca held out a handful
of nuts saying, "Oh, Tewa Tewa,
you must be hungry."

"You are so generous, Prisca!"

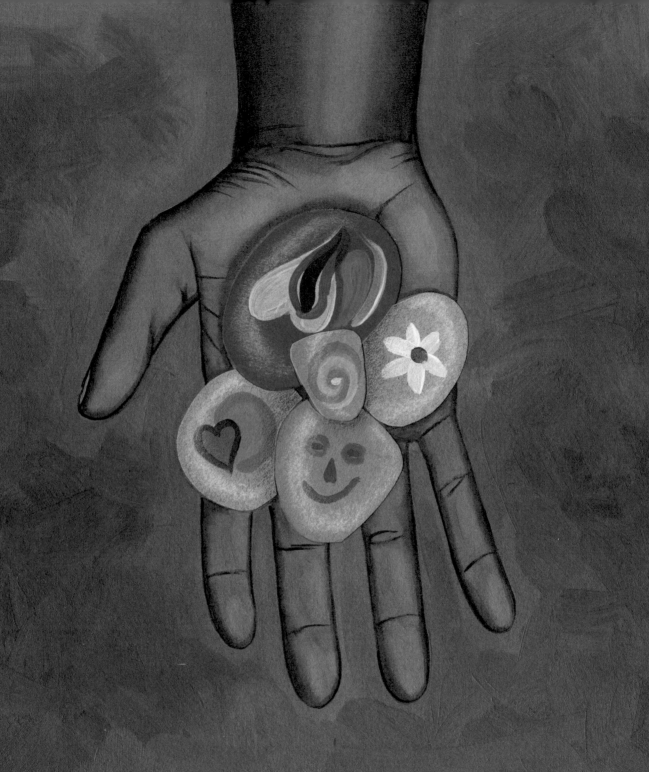

Then he handed her back the stones.

"I'm sorry, Prisca. I couldn't sell any."

"Well," said Prisca, not ready to give up, "How about paper bead necklaces?"

"Make some and we'll see," said Tewa Tewa.

"I will," Prisca cried. "Here I come, Caleb!"

She found the shiny paper she and Caleb had saved for a special day. She cut it just right, rolled each piece tight, and strung all the paper beads together.

The next day when Tewa Tewa came, she held them up with delight.

But later that day, he returned with the same necklaces. "I'm sorry, Prisca. I couldn't sell any."

"Well," said Prisca. "How about corn husk dolls?"

"Make some and we'll see," said Tewa Tewa.

"I will! *Ow, ow, ooowww*!" Prisca howled her joyful howl.

She gathered husks from the field and soaked them soft, just like Caleb had taught her. She folded and trimmed and added tassels of hair. While she worked, she imagined how happy Caleb would be to see her.

He'd dance around her and laugh his raucous laugh, "*Heee, hee, hee, heeee!*"

"Prisca, they're lovely!" Tewa Tewa exclaimed.
She tied them tall and proud to his handlebars.

But that day it rained till the ground turned to floods of red mud.

Prisca called, "Tewa Tewa, come here where it's dry."

She handed him a cloth to wipe his face.

"You are so caring, Prisca!" Tewa Tewa said.

Then she reached for
her dolls, all splattered with
mud, and they fell apart in
her hands.

"Iyayi! I'll never see
Caleb."

She ran through the rain, slipping through mud,
her "*ow, ow, ooowww*" joyful howl sounding more like a whimper.

All through the rainy season she carried water, washed clothes, ground corn, and swept the yard, always thinking of Caleb.

He'd be older and smarter, but their love would still be as big as the sky.

Then one day Tewa Tewa came by on a bicycle that was bare.

"What happened?" cried Prisca.

"My bike needed fixing."

She studied his bike and then said, "Tewa Tewa, do you think *you* could take Mama and me to see Caleb?"

"Me?" he exclaimed. "On this?"

He paced back and forth, thinking.

Then he said, "Prisca, you give me water when I'm thirsty, food when I'm hungry, and shelter when I'm drenched. Now I'll do something for you. I'll take you and your mama to see Caleb."

Mama frowned. "Can we make it that far?"

"We'll make it!" Tewa Tewa laughed.

Prisca howled with joy, "*Ow, ow, ooowww!*"

They piled together on the bike that barely held them and sped down bumpy roads that made their teeth chatter. They wobbled past mud huts and trading tents, tipped and swerved around oxcarts, dodged women balancing baskets, and children chasing chickens.

They jiggled and bounced and stirred up the ground till they were sneezing and coughing and covered with dust.

After hours of pedaling, Tewa Tewa moaned, "Ndatopa. My legs can pump no more."

"Please, just a bit farther," Prisca cried.

Finally, they spotted the brick dwellings of Chimwe sprawled across the valley below.

"Prisca!" Caleb cried, racing toward her.

They spun round and round, till they were dizzy with delight.

And together they tumbled to the ground.

"*Heee, hee, hee, heeee!*" Caleb laughed his raucous laugh.

"*Ow, ow, ooowww!*" Prisca howled her joyful howl.

He was her feisty brother and she was his spunky

sister, and their love was *still* as big as the sky.

And it always would be.